# THE PARABLE OF TWO BUILDERS

## A Retelling of the Bible Story

Written by
**MELODY CARLSON**

Illustrated by
**STEVE BJÖRKMAN**

Zonderkidz

*The Parable of Two Builders*
ISBN  0-310-70145-7
Copyright © 1998 by Zondervan
Illustrations © 1998 by Steve Björkman

Requests for information should be addressed to:

Zonder**kidz**™

*The children's group of Zondervan*

Grand Rapids, Michigan 49530
www.zonderkidz.com

*The Parable of Two Builders* was previously published by Gold 'n' Honey Books, a division of Multnomah Publishers, Inc.
Zonderkidz is a trademark of Zondervan.

Written by: Melody Carlson
Interior Design by D2 Designworks

Printed in China
02 03 04 05/HK/5 4 3 2 1

To Chris,
May you always build on the
Rock that never moves.
With love,
mc

To Lee, Susan & Andy.
With love,
sb

Both these two men have a job to do,
A house to build, and to live in too.
One will choose to build it right.
But the other will have a horrible fright.
A fright!
That's right!
One will not build it right!

Meet this man, his name is Nick.
He wants a house—he wants it quick!
And so he builds right on the sand.
He says, "No problem, this house will stand."
To stand?
On sand?
Nick does not understand.

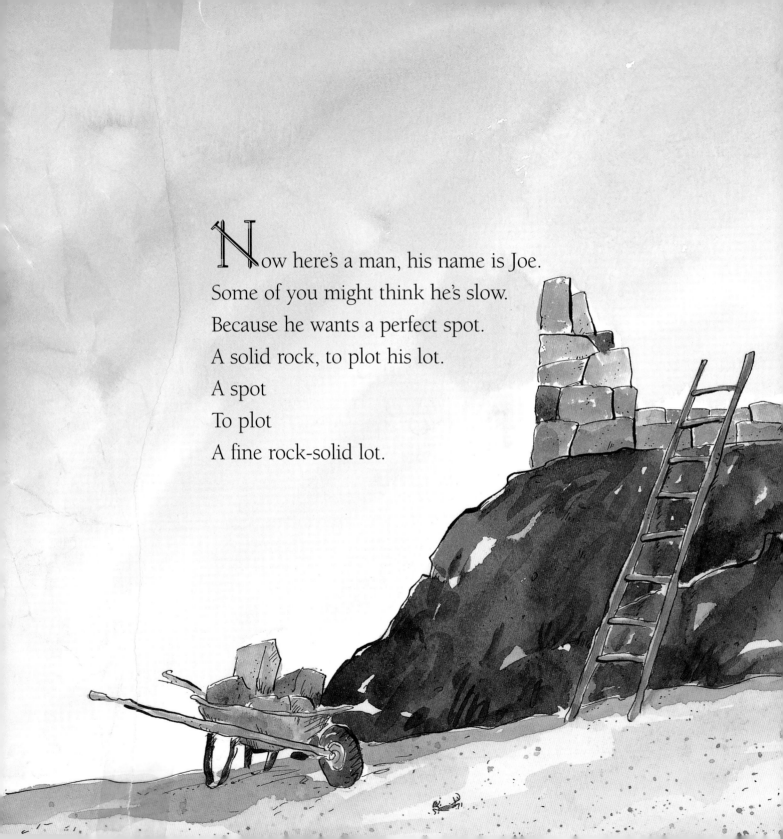

Now here's a man, his name is Joe.
Some of you might think he's slow.
Because he wants a perfect spot.
A solid rock, to plot his lot.
A spot
To plot
A fine rock-solid lot.

**W**ell, Nick is fast, Nick is quick.

He builds his house of fancy brick.

His roof is made of finest tile.

And he steps back with a big smile.

He smiles

A while.

But only for a while.

Joe is working—all alone.

It's not easy to build on stone.

He takes his time, he does it right.

Sometimes he works into the night.

That's right!

All night.

But Joe will do it right.

Neighbors come, and it is fun,
To see Nick's house in the bright sun.
Nick paints his trim perky pink.
And when he's done, it makes him blink.
He blinks
At pink
But does not stop to think.

Joe works hard—and carefully.
Sometimes he even works prayerfully.
At last, at last—he's finally done!
He watches his house in the setting sun.
He's done!
He's done!
And now he'll have some fun!

The next day, Nick sees the sky.
He runs inside and says, "Oh my!"
No sooner does he close the door
Than those black clouds begin to pour.
They pour.
And pour.
And then they pour some more.

Z Z Z Z Z Z Z

Joe's in his house—safe and sound.
He knows it's built on solid ground.
He hears the rain, he hears it pour.
He goes to sleep—and he does snore!
It pours.
Joe snores.
And then he snores some more!

Nick is worried, Nick feels sick.

Maybe he built his house too quick.

Maybe it's true, a house won't stand

When it's built upon the sand.

Won't stand

On sand

This wasn't what Nick planned.

The storm is nasty, it is wild!
Big winds blow, and waves get riled!
Flood waters rise, and start to splash!
Lightning strike! And thunder crash!
Boom bash!
Big crash!
Flood waters make a splash!

Things look bad, Nick sees trouble.
Soon his house will turn to rubble.
He watches as it falls ker-splat!
Tumbling down, until it's flat!
Ker-splat!
It's flat!
It's gone, and that is that!

The next morning, Joe gets up,
He goes outside to walk his pup.
Last night's storm sure was rough.
But the rock-hard house still stands tough.
It's tough
Enough
To face the fiercest stuff.

Joe is worried for his friend,
Could this storm have been his end?
He hurries to the sorry sight,
And finds poor Nick in a big fright.
A fright!
A sight!
Thank goodness, Nick's all right!

Nick says to Joe, "I understand.
I see it's foolish to build on sand.
I'll build on rock, just like you do,
A house that's solid and right and true.
I'll do
Like you
On a rock that's solid and true."

Joe helped Nick. It didn't take long,

To find a rock—big and strong.

And if you're smart you'll find One too.

And build your life on the One who's true.

He's true

To you.

And He will see you through.

"Some people come to me and listen to me and do what I say. I will show you what they are like. They are like someone who builds a house. He digs down deep and sets it on solid rock. When a flood comes, the river rushes against the house. But the water can't shake it. The house is well built. But here is what happens when people listen to my words and do not obey them. They are like someone who builds a house on soft ground instead of solid rock. The moment the river rushes against that house, it falls down. It is completely destroyed."

LUKE 6:47–49 (NIrV)